10/29/01

Tiny Tours Bermuda's Ocean
Another Tree Frog Adventure

Illustrated and written by
Elizabeth A. Mulderig

Designed by David Conrad

Published by
The Bermudian Publishing Company Limited
P.O. Box HM 283
Hamilton HM AX
Bermuda

Printed in Singapore

First Published 1993
Reprinted 1996

ISBN   976-8104-57-0

The **Tree Frog** (*Eleutherodatylus johnstonei*) is among the most well-known features of Bermuda nightlife. As the sun sets and dampness falls, the tree frog's high-pitched 'gleep' begins to fill the night air. The sound is a result of the frogs talking to each other from high in a tree or under a garden rock. Although the frog is not indigenous to Bermuda, it has become a 'native' as it would not be a true Bermuda night without its distinctive sound. Most tree frogs sleep through the day. Most, that is, except Tiny...

With love to the 'picnic on the moon gang':
Kaitlin, Meghan, Drew, and James

Special thanks to my family, Richard Winchell, Patricia, David, and Kevin.

Tiny the tree frog
Decided one day
To explore the ocean
In his own special way.

Salt water is not
Where most tree frogs swim
But Tiny was different
From the rest of his kin.

So he took a leap
Right into the bay
To tour a big ocean
The Bermudian way.

On his own again
Tiny swam down deep
And announced he was there
With a small muffled 'gleep'.

Under the water
The world was so blue
It bedazzled Tiny
And a parrot fish, too!

A swinging seahorse
Swam in with the tide
Tiny hopped on her back
Holding pearls for the ride.

Swimming down deeper
Presented no strain
He came upon coral
That resembled a brain.

A lobster chilled out
Behind a tall fan
A guinea chick dude
Dressed in hot pink and tan.

The hamlet grouper
Was prince of the sea
Still, he would ask
"To be or not to be?"

Then floating on by
Came a ghostly thing
Oops! It was a 'fish'
Who knew how to sting.

Tiny swam upwards
For some air at last
A tangle of seaweed
Sent him swimming down fast.

But he continued
Brave and undaunted
'Til he saw a wreck
That seemed to be haunted.

Swimming back quickly
To change direction
Tiny found a sea egg
For prickly protection.

On the coral sand
He saw a conch shell
Along with a starfish
Didn't Tiny do well?

The sea plants that grew
Looked strange to our boy
The flopsy, mopsy one
Being shy and quite coy.

A sergeant major
Named Bubbles Bernard
Saluted to Tiny
While swimming on guard.

He paddled through
A school of small fish
And sent them scuttling
As his big feet went swish!

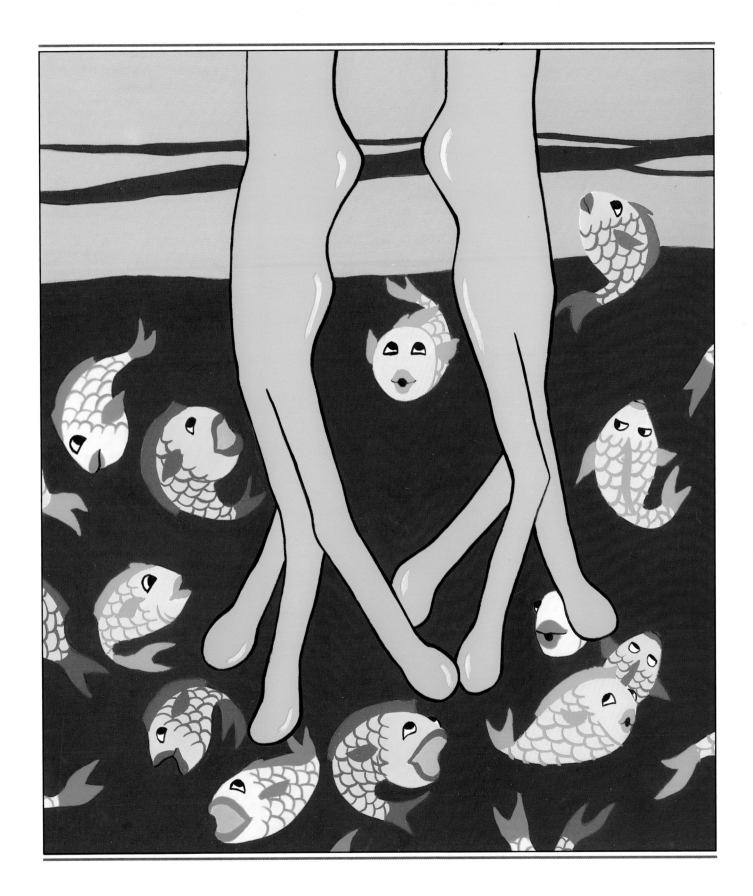

Next there were turtles
Eating 'turtle grass'
With no table manners
Tiny thought they were crass.

Things underwater
Could flip Tiny's lid
Including those odd
Little back-swimming squid.

He yucked up a pearl
From its sea shell bed
But as Tiny rose up
The jewel tumbled instead.

Tiny never knew
A rock could conceal
A huge slimy creature
Like a green moray eel.

Suddenly he felt
His homeland calling
He was lonely again
And night-time was falling.

When he looked round
He knew he was lost
But along came a wave
And poor Tiny was tossed.

Back to his ace boys
Who caught him mid-air
To hear the adventures
Tiny told with great flair.